THE LITTLE CIRCLE

THE LITTLE CIRCLE

Text and photographs
by Ann Atwood

Charles Scribner's Sons / New York

TO

Joan and Michael

who made the little circle

complete

A—10.67 [RH]
Printed in the United States of America
Library of Congress Catalog Card Number 67-24045

The first thing the Little Circle remembered was being drawn on a blackboard by a piece of chalk.

"And this is a zero!" someone was saying.

"And a zero is Nothing!" piped a small high voice.

This is how the Little Circle learned he was a zero, and that a zero is nothing.

He felt sad and empty, and he thought about it for a long time. Then he had a very good idea.

"Everything has to be *something*," he reasoned. "It is only a matter of finding out what that something is."

So the Little Circle dropped bravely down from the blackboard and out into the spring morning to find out what he was.

Soon he saw a child rolling a hoop across a hill. At the sight of the hoop he had a strange and lovely feeling.

"I must hurry and catch up with it!" he thought. With all the speed he could manage he drew up beside it.

"Wait!" he called.

"What do you want?" asked the hoop.

"I'm trying to find myself," said the Little Circle breathlessly.

The hoop nodded. "Stretch yourself out and slip inside me," it said.

When the Little Circle did, he was surprised to find that every part of him fit cosily inside the round body of the hoop with nothing left over.

"Am I a hoop?" he asked in amazement.

"Yes," replied the hoop.

So the Little Circle looped down the path. The wind rushed through him, and the tall mustard blurred past him.

Dizzy with happiness, he sang a song to his shadow running beside him:

> *Who's small on the outside*
> *And big on the inside?*
> *Who's soft in the middle*
> *And hard on the thinside?*

"I am!" sang the Little Circle.

He was slowing down when he saw a
tree straight in front of him. There was a
jolting crash, and the Little Circle was hurled
through the air and thrown into the grass.
In another minute he could see the hoop,
bent and shapeless, lying under the tree.

"I am no longer a hoop," he thought sadly. He wanted to cry, but just then he heard a cheery voice high above him. He looked up into a round golden face.

"I am a daisy," said the face, smiling. "Won't you come in?" And the Little Circle pressed himself inside. He was too sore and tired to notice what a snug fit it was. He only knew he felt warm and spongy as he fell asleep.

While he slept he dreamed he could make himself into anything at all. When he woke he began to stir, but there was no room in which to move.

"Am I a daisy?" he asked.

"Yes," said the flower.

"Then I am a hoop *and* a daisy," said the Little Circle in wonder.

"Of course, and that is only the beginning!" promised the daisy.

"Then I can't stay any longer," said the Little Circle. "I must hurry if I am going to find out all the things I am."

And he eased himself gently out of the flower so he would not leave a dent in its soft, round rim.

He wheeled along, humming as he went:

> *Who runs like a hoop?*
> *Who sleeps in a flower?*
> *Who's likely to be*
> *Something else in an hour?*

"I am!" sang the Little Circle.

And in even less than an hour the Little Circle came to a lovely garden. Patches of purple and gold flowers spread through the lawns. In the distance water was falling over a ledge. The Little Circle tilted through trees and hedges till he came to a fountain.

"Play with me!" the fountain called.
Reaching it, the Little Circle looked
deep down into a pool of dancing diamonds.

Around the diamonds a ripple was spinning. And around that ripple swirled another ripple, and around it another. Each ring was wider and larger than the last. They all shimmered in the sun.

The Little Circle could scarcely contain himself.

"I must be a ripple," he thought. But just to be sure, he decided to try the smallest ripple first.

The moment he slipped into it he felt light as a cork. He could sway and dip and turn with no effort at all.

For a long time he splashed and spun. Then he slid boldly into the next ripple. Although it was bigger, it was not as lively as the first. He bobbed gently up and down, singing his riddle:

> *Who sleeps in a daisy?*
> *Who rolls down a mountain?*
> *Who's round as a ripple*
> *And plays in a fountain?*

"I do!" sang the Little Circle.

The sun warmed him. He was airy and very sure of himself. So he tried all the ripples. The larger they were, the quieter they became.

He was floating lazily on the last and widest ring when it began to slip out from under him. It went down, down, down into the water. The Little Circle just had time to reach the edge of the pool and tip himself over into the thick grass.

It was soft and green, but it wasn't grass. It was gliding slowly through the shade, and the Little Circle was gliding with it. He was surrounded by dazzling jewels. Cool blue sapphires turned to bright green emeralds as they drifted out of the shadows into the sun. Each gem was set in glistening gold.

"Who are you?" he asked in astonishment.

The jewel nearest him replied, "I am the eye of a peacock's tail."

"What's the eye of a peacock's tail?" questioned the Little Circle.

"A beautiful thing," said a voice. And that satisfied the Little Circle, for he was gazing in wonder at the jeweled eye. The colors in its center were changing from green to purple and then to silver-blue. He longed to sink down into the gold velvet oval around it.

"Am I the eye of a peacock's tail?" he whispered.

"Not quite," it answered, "but almost."

"Almost . . ." echoed the Little Circle.

He felt like singing a sad song, and he felt like singing a glad song both at the same time. But he couldn't think of any words for the song he wanted to sing.

Then with no warning he felt himself rising. The branch of a tree was coming closer and closer. As the peacock's feathers fluttered in the wind, the Little Circle was tossed into the tree. Swinging his way along the branch, he tumbled into a small, tight nest. It was made of twigs and grasses. It smelled of sunshine.

"Welcome!" it said.

And indeed he felt welcome, for he nestled neatly into it.

"I am a nest," he said aloud, for he didn't even have to ask. This time he was sure. The baby birds he was holding lay in the shadows, fast asleep.

The Little Circle was so content he decided to take a nap. But first he looked down to see where the peacock had flown. It was sitting in a nearby tree, its long tail rippling down.

The Little Circle thought of a wistful riddle:

Who has gold and emerald rings?
Who has magic-carpet wings?
Who is one of the beautiful things?

"I am . . . almost," sighed the Little Circle.

And then he went to sleep.

The loud, hungry cries of the baby birds awakened him. The mother bird was dropping worms into their large, open mouths. The Little Circle yawned and stretched. Being a nest gave him a safe and sleepy feeling, but he was ready to go on.

"Good-bye, little sparrows," he said. "Soon you will be leaving too." And he shifted himself over onto a branch.

He wasn't sure how he was going to get down, so he settled in the crotch of the tree until he could think of something.

As he was thinking, he saw a small dot in the sky. It was coming toward him, and as it came it got bigger and bigger. Then he saw that it was red and round. It fluttered into the branch beside him. As it bumped the branch, the leaves held it fast. The smooth red ball came to a stop.

"Hello there!" said the Little Circle. "Who are you, and what are you doing here?"

"Nothing I *want* to be doing," sighed a breezy voice. "For you see, I'm a balloon."

The Little Circle was looking intently at the red ball.

"I, too, am a balloon!' he announced excitedly. "I'll ride with you." And he leaned toward it.

"Carefully, carefully," warned the balloon. "I am very fragile."

So the Little Circle fitted himself cautiously around the balloon. It quivered, but just enough to free itself. Then they were sailing away into the sky.

The Little Circle looked down at the tops of the trees.

"I have come a long way from being nothing," he thought. And he felt like singing a riddle about the balloon:

> *There's nobody near it*
> *To steer it*
> *Or spin it*
> *Yet who can fly*
> > *To the sky*
> > > *In a minute?*

"I can!" sang the Little Circle.

He bounced softly in the wind as the balloon rose higher and higher.

Below him a roller-coaster fence dipped up and down over the green hills. He was light as the clouds floating with him.

After a while, a sea gull flew under him. Looking down, he

saw a wide, white beach. He was almost over it when the Little Circle felt himself growing smaller and smaller.

As he grew smaller, he began to fall. Faster and faster he dropped, parachuting down to land on the sandy beach. He looked all around for the balloon, but he couldn't find it anywhere.

Something wet and very strong was pulling and pushing him. He was swept into the sea and barely able to keep his shape.

Before he knew it, he was floating in the water. A long, silvery wave was riding toward him. It was the most magnificent thing he had ever seen. As it began to curve, the Little Circle began to hope . . .

"Am I the sea?" he whispered to himself.

Then he heard a thundering roar. He was tossed up on a rock covered with sea grass. He didn't even notice the lovely colors and shapes in the tide pool near him. All he could think of was the powerful comber. More than anything in the world he now longed to be the sea.

"Good day!" someone was saying.

The Little Circle did not feel like talking to anyone.

"Why don't you come in awhile?" the voice went on.

The Little Circle turned to look. A spiny, purple pincushion was sitting in the sea grass beside him. Any other day it would have started him singing the song of himself, but today it was small comfort.

"Don't you want to be a sea urchin?" asked the voice.

"Forgive me," said the Little Circle. "I didn't mean to be rude." And he slid inside. It was a smooth room with a lavendar dome. It was cool and welcoming.

"It is very pretty here," said the Little Circle. Then he hastened to explain: "It is just that I want to be the sea *so much* that I can't think of anything else." And while the sea urchin was sunning, he slipped quietly out so as not to disturb his new friend.

A great breaker was rolling in near a cave. As it arched its back, the Little Circle held his breath. Just as it was about to curl itself over into a green globe, it crashed!

"Not quite . . . " sighed the Little Circle. And the cave behind the breaker echoed, "Not quite . . . "

Evening was coming on, and the Little Circle waited as close to the ocean as he dared. The edge of the white water pushed up against him, and drew back. Sadly he watched the sea leaving strips of foam on the shore.

Then, suddenly the sand was gleaming with tiny bubbles, blue and green and purple and rose. As they broke, they made a tinkling sound, like the sound of faint and faraway bells. Each one was chiming, "Come and sing with me!"

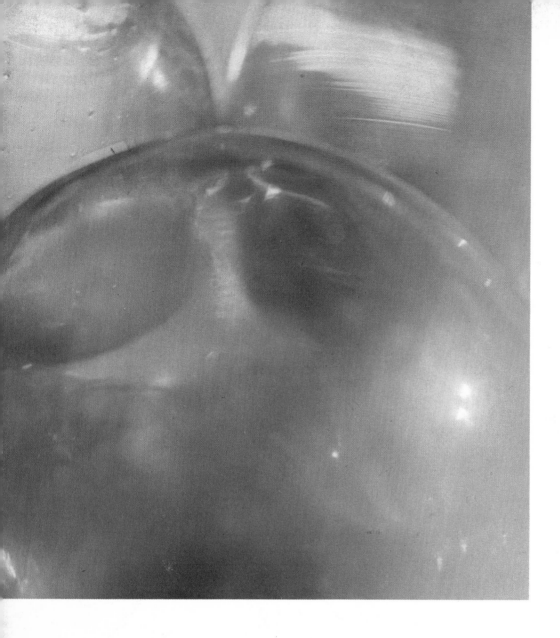

The Little Circle felt a tingling of joy. He squeezed inside the one nearest to him. Through the mist he could see the others twinkling like rainbows. He felt filmy and moist.

"I *am* the sea!" he cried, scarcely believing it.

Above him clouds were drifting in. As he looked from shore to sky, the Little Circle saw the round, gold sun. The song inside him grew louder and louder.

So he began to sing a new riddle. And it was longer than any riddle he had ever sung before:

Who whirls like a top?
Who's soft as a daisy?
Who holds baby sparrows?
Who's red, round and lazy?

Who's shiny
And spiny
And covered with foam?
Who has a window
Of rainbows
At home?

Who's the moon
Flying free?
Who's the sun
And the sea?

"ME!" answered the Little Circle.